IMAGINE THAT™

Licensed exclusively to Imagine That Publishing Ltd
Tide Mill Way, Woodbridge, Suffolk, IP12 1AP, UK
www.imaginethat.com
Copyright © 2019 Imagine That Group Ltd
All rights reserved
2 4 6 8 9 7 5 3 1
Manufactured in China

Written by Susie Linn
Illustrated by Parwinder Singh

ISBN 978-1-78958-305-2

A catalogue record for this book is available from the British Library

Star Light Star Bright

Susie Linn
Parwinder Singh

Star light, star bright,
The first star I see tonight,
I wish I may, I wish I might,
Have the wish I wish tonight.

Star light, star bright,
A wish I wish to make tonight.

I'd like my friend to come to stay,
And play with me for one whole day!

Star light, star bright,
A wish I wish to make tonight.

I'd love a bike to ride and race,
Around the park, from place to place.

Star light, star bright,
A wish I wish to make tonight.

10:15

A day with Mum and Dad, alone,
A great day out, or fun at home.

Star light, star bright,
A wish I wish to make tonight.

Big snowflakes fall while I'm asleep,
All bright and cold and very deep!

Star light, star bright,
A wish I wish to make tonight.

Make me strong so I can climb,
Up that big hill, time after time.

Star light, star bright,
A wish I wish to make tonight.
A superhero I will be,
Super-smart – hey, look at me!

Star light, star bright,
A wish I wish to make tonight.

I wish my birthday would come soon,
With party fun and big balloons!

Star light, star bright,
A wish I wish to make tonight.
A teddy bear, all fur and paws,
For play inside or play outdoors.

Star light, star bright,
A wish I wish to make tonight.

A windy day, my kite to fly,
And see it soaring, way up high!

Star light, star bright,
A wish I wish to make tonight.
A day full of my favourite treats,
My perfect things to do and eat!

Star light, star bright,
A wish I wish to make tonight.

That shooting stars will come my way,
To wish on every single day!